ANNA'S PET

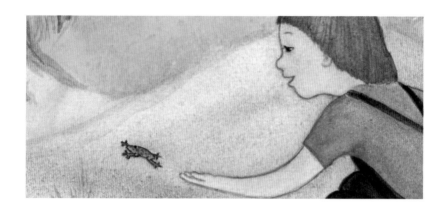

MARGARET ATWOOD
JOYCE BARKHOUSE

ILLUSTRATED BY ANN BLADES

LORIMER

JAMES LORIMER & COMPANY LTD., PUBLISHERS
TORONTO

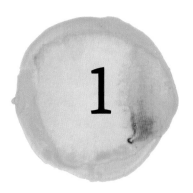

1

"Hello, Anna," said Grandma. "We've often come to visit you in the city. Now you have come to visit us."

"Come and we'll show you our farm," said Grandpa. "You can see our pond and all our cows."

Anna had never seen so much grass and so many cows.

"I'd like to have a pet," she said to Grandpa. "I don't have a pet at home. Could I have one of your cows?"

"Oh, Anna," said Grandpa, laughing. "A cow is too big for a pet. But look around. Maybe you'll find something smaller."

Anna looked on the ground near the pond. She found a little toad and picked it up.

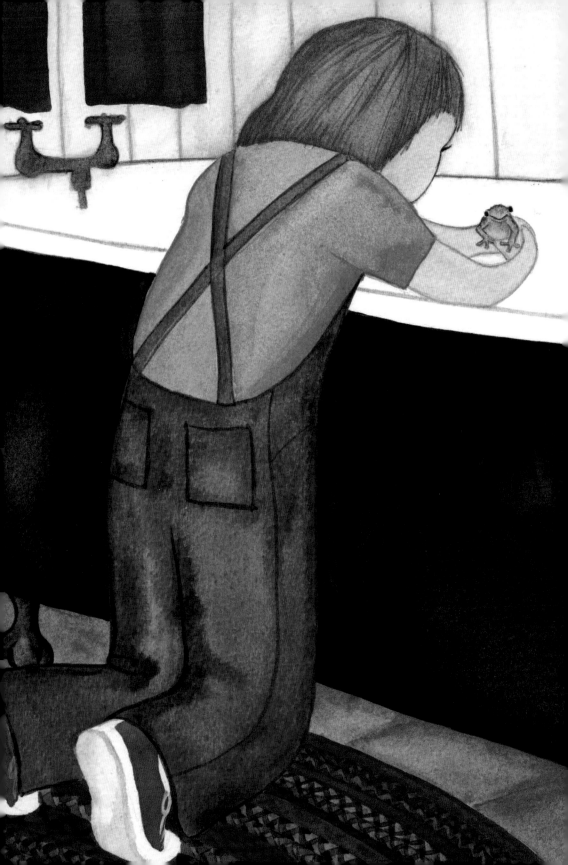

"This toad can be my pet," said Anna.

"What do toads like?" she wondered. "Maybe they like water."

Anna carried the toad into the house. She took it to the bathtub and filled the bathtub with water. Then she put the toad into the bathtub.

"There, little toad," she said. "Swim around and have fun."

Grandma came into the bathroom. "Hello, Anna," she said. "Are you going to have a bath?"

"No," said Anna. "My toad is having a bath. This toad is my pet."

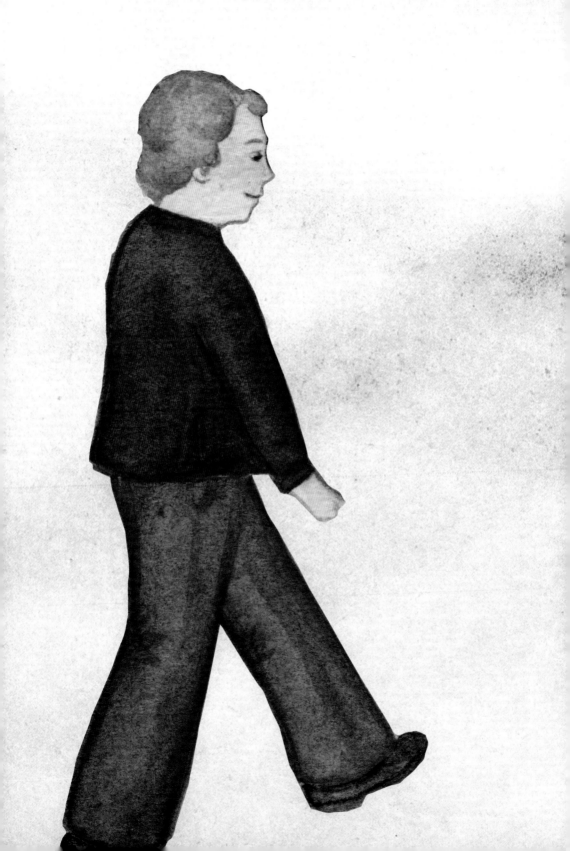

Grandma looked at the toad. Then she picked it up. "This toad doesn't look happy," she said. "I don't think toads like bathtubs."

"What do toads like?" asked Anna.

"Toads like it where it's dark and cool," said Grandma. "They don't like to stay in the water all the time. Toads aren't the same as frogs."

"Where do toads live?" asked Anna.

"Toads live under things," said Grandma. "Sometimes they live under logs. As long as it's cool and dark and under something, a toad will like it."

"I know why this toad didn't like the bathtub," said Anna. "It's too bright and too warm, and it's not under anything."

"Yes," said Grandma. "You should put the toad where it will be happy."

"All right," said Anna. "I do want a pet, but I don't want one if it's unhappy."

Anna took the toad back to the pond. She put it down and the toad hopped away.

"Goodbye, toad," she said. "I hope you find a home that is cool and dark and under something. I want you to be happy."

2

Anna was still looking for a pet. She wanted something small that she could hold. She looked in the garden and she found a little pink worm.

Anna picked the worm up. At first it wiggled, but then it was still.

"What a nice worm," said Anna. "You can be my pet. But I must find a home for you."

She stopped to think. "What do worms like? Maybe they like the same things toads like. I'll find a place that's cool and dark and under something."

Anna went into the house.

"Maybe I should put my worm in the refrigerator," she said. "It's cool and dark — oh, but it's not really under anything."

Then Anna went upstairs. "Maybe I should put my worm in the closet," she said. Anna looked in the closet. "It's too warm in here."

"I know," she said. "I'll put my worm under Grandpa and Grandma's bed. It's cool and dark there."

Anna put the worm under Grandpa and Grandma's bed. "There, little worm," she said. "You'll be happy now."

Anna ran to tell Grandma about her new pet worm. At the door she bumped into Grandpa.

"Hello, Anna," he said. "What are you doing?"

"Hello, Grandpa," said Anna. "I put a worm under your bed."

"Oh," said Grandpa. "You put a worm under my bed, did you? Are you playing a joke on me?"

"Oh, no," said Anna. "That's my worm's new home. It's cool and dark and under something. Toads like places like that, so worms must like them too."

"Oh, Anna! A worm isn't the same as a toad," said Grandpa. He looked under the bed and pulled out the worm. It was covered with dust.

"This worm doesn't look happy," he said. "Worms don't like being under beds."

"What do worms like?" asked Anna.

"Worms like it where it's cool and dark, just like toads," said Grandpa. "But they like to live in the earth. Earth isn't the same as dust. Dust is dry and earth is damp."

"I know why the worm didn't like it under your bed," said Anna. "It was too dry. And there wasn't any earth."

"That's right," said Grandpa. "You should put the worm where it will be happy."

Anna took the worm outside to the garden. She put it down and the worm wiggled away.

"Goodbye, worm," said Anna. "I hope you find a home. Dig a tunnel in the earth. Then you'll be happy."

3

Anna still wanted a pet.

She looked in Grandma's rock garden and saw something wiggling. It was a little green snake.

Anna caught it. When she picked it up, the snake curled around her hand. It felt dry and cool.

Anna said, "This snake can move very fast. I'm going to put it in a pail."

Anna found one of Grandpa's pails and put the snake in it. The snake could not get out.

"But what do snakes like?" Anna wondered. "A snake is long, like a worm. Worms and snakes don't have any feet. Worms and snakes don't have any hair. Maybe snakes like to live in the earth, just like worms."

So Anna put some earth in on top of the snake.

Then Grandpa came out of the barn.

"Hello, Anna," he said. "What are you doing with my pail?"

"I have a pet snake," said Anna. "I'm making a home for it. It will dig a hole in this earth, just like a worm."

Grandpa laughed. "Oh, Anna! A snake isn't like a worm. That snake won't like being covered with earth. It won't be happy."

"What do snakes like, then?" asked Anna.

"Snakes like it where it's hot and dry," said Grandpa.

So Anna took the snake out of the pail and ran to the house. She went into the kitchen.

"Hello, Anna," said Grandma. "What do you have now?"

"This is my new pet snake," said Anna. "Snakes like places where it's hot and dry. So I'm going to put my snake into the oven."

"No, no," said Grandma. "If you put it into the oven, you will cook it."

"I don't want to cook the snake," said Anna. "I want to make a home for it."

"Snakes don't live inside the house," said Grandma.

Anna was sad. "Where do snakes live?" she asked.

"Come with me," said Grandma. "I'll show you where snakes live."

Grandma and Anna went outside. Grandma put the snake into the garden.

"This is where the snake lives," she said. "In the daytime, when it's sunny, the snake can come out and lie on the rock. At night, when it's cool, the snake can go down between the rocks. This is the best home for a snake."

"Goodbye, snake," said Anna. "I see that you like your home. It's a better place for you than a pail or a house. You will be happy here."

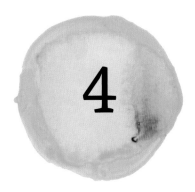

4

Anna stood in the garden feeling sad. She still didn't have a pet.

"I found a toad," she said. "I found a worm, and I found a snake. But none of them liked the homes I made for them. Maybe I'll never find a pet."

Just then Grandma walked by.

"Hello, Anna," she said. "Are you feeling sad?"

"Yes, Grandma," said Anna "I'm sad because I don't have a pet and I really want one. Something I can watch. Something little that I can take back to the city. Something that will be happy."

"Come with me," said Grandma. "I know where we can find a pet for you."

Grandma and Anna went down to the pond. Grandma took off her shoes and rolled up her pants and her sleeves. Then she put a pail in the water.

"Here, Anna," she said. "Here's a pet for you."

Anna looked into the pail. "What is it?" she asked.

"It's a tadpole," said Grandma. "It can live in a big jar of water. You can take it back to the city."

"A tadpole is a little black fish," said Anna. "I don't want a fish. I want a pet I can hold in my hands."

Grandma laughed. "No, Anna, a tadpole isn't a fish. It's a very strange thing. It will grow into something very different. Now we'll make a home for your new pet."

Grandma found a big jar and put some sand and water in it. Then she emptied the bucket and the tadpole into the jar. Anna watched the tadpole. It swam very fast.

But Anna wasn't happy yet.

"I still think a tadpole is a fish. I think you're playing a joke on me, Grandma," she said.

Just then Grandpa came in. He looked at the jar.

"Oh, you have a tadpole! Do you know what will happen? First it will grow legs and feet. Then it will grow arms and hands, and its tail will disappear. Your tadpole will turn into a baby frog."

Anna laughed. "A baby frog! Oh, good! I'll be able to hold it in my hands and watch it jump."

"Yes, but you can't keep the baby frog very long," said Grandma. "You must bring it back to the pond and let it go. The pond is its home."

"All right," said Anna. "Thank you, Grandma. I like this tadpole very much. I'll take it back to the city and watch it grow. But I wish I could keep it forever."

"I know," said Grandma. "But it's hard to keep anything forever."

The End.

James Lorimer & Company Ltd., Publishers acknowledges the support of
the Ontario Arts Council. We acknowledge the financial support of the
Government of Canada through the Canada Book Fund for our publishing
activities. We acknowledge the support of the Canada Council for the Arts
which last year invested $20.1 million in writing and publishing throughout
Canada. We acknowledge the Government of Ontario through the Ontario
Media Development Corporation's Ontario Book Initiative.

Library and Archives Canada Cataloguing in Publication

Atwood, Margaret, 1939-
          Anna's pet / Margaret Atwood, Joyce Barkhouse ; illustrated by Ann Blades.

ISBN 978-1-55277-718-3

          I. Barkhouse, Joyce, 1913- II. Blades, Ann, 1947 III. Title.

PS8501.T86A88 2011   jC813'.54   C2010-907942-6

James Lorimer & Company Ltd., Publishers
317 Adelaide Street West, Suite #1002
Toronto, Ontario, Canada M5V 1P9
www.lorimer.ca

Distributed in the United States by:
Orca Book Publishers
P.O. Box 468
Custer, WA USA
98240-0468

Printed and bound by Everbest Printing Company Ltd. in Guangzhou, China in
April 2011.
Job#: 99876